# The Desert Island

by

## Morgan Georgia Blanks

### Illustrations by Sussi Arctander

*AuthorHouse™ UK Ltd.*
*500 Avebury Boulevard*
*Central Milton Keynes, MK9 2BE*
*www.authorhouse.co.uk*
*Phone: 08001974150*

*First published by AuthorHouse 11/8/2008*

*ISBN: 978-1-4343-9006-6 (sc)*

*Printed in the United States of America*
*Bloomington, Indiana*

*This book is printed on acid-free paper.*

authorHOUSE®

Once there was a desert island, far, far away…..
in the middle of nowhere.

# Chapter 1
# The New Boat

On a small piece of land just outside the little Cornish seaside village of Smugleton, there was a cottage, and in that cottage lived a man and a woman and their son Jack.

Jack loved to play on the beach near his cottage. He used to stand, looking out to the horizon. He wanted to know what was out there, in the middle of nowhere, out at sea.

"Mum, do you know if there's a piece of land in the middle of nowhere?" asked Jack.

'I don't know' she answered.

"What's that Jack?" said his father.

'Don't worry' said Jack.

His father looked curious.

"He wants to know if there's a piece of land in the middle of nowhere" said Jack's mum.

Jack said nothing and went outside. He looked out to the sea, the wind blowing in his face. Oh how he'd love to know what was out there.

Suddenly he saw a wreck washed up against the shore.

"A boat!" cried Jack, and he rushed over to it. He peered curiously at it and suddenly had an idea!!

He ran back to the shed in the garden and picked up some wood, some nails and his Dad's hammer.

"I'm going to build this wreck back into a wonderful boat" he said cheerfully, "then I can go sailing!"

Jack worked all day on his boat until it was time for bed. The next morning he got up early and finally finished it. He made a big flag which he put on top of the mast. It said 'JACK'S BOAT'.

"Perfect!!" said Jack and he packed some food and drink in his back pack before he went off to the beach.

Jack pushed the boat into the water and set off. The sun shone brightly as Jack set sail, the waves whooshing up against the boat.

Jack took a banana out of his bag and ate it.

Suddenly the sky turned black and it started raining. "Oh no!"

He started rowing, fast. He didn't want to get caught in the rain.

He climbed the mast to look for land. In the distance, he spotted what looked like a small island. "I must get shelter" he said, and sailed towards it.

As soon as he got there he realized that no one had been here before. "WOW" gasped Jack, "it's a desert Island!".

Jack decided to explore the Island. He saw palm trees, coconuts and lots more exciting things.

At the end of the island, Jack found some shelter.

"Oh, I'm hungry" he said and took out some food from his bag to eat.

He soon realized that he really was in the middle of nowhere. Suddenly, he heard a sound behind him…......

# Chapter 2
# On the Island

"Who's there" said Jack, scared. "What's that sound?"

'It's me', said a tearful voice behind him.

Jack turned and saw a sad looking monkey. She had a little red bow in her hair.

"What's wrong?" said Jack.

'My island's wrong' replied the monkey.

"Your island?" said Jack,

'Yes, my island' said the monkey, looking saddened.

"Well, my name's Jack, and I'm from England!"

'Pleased to meet you Jack, my name is Laura, and I live here!'

"Sorry I had to come to your island and shelter from the rain" Jack said.

'Don't worry' said Laura, and she smiled at him.

While they were talking, the rain had eased and the sky brightened, just a little. They both sat on the beach, watching the dark clouds as they drifted away.

"Why were you crying?" asked Jack, "what's wrong with your island?"

'It's sinking. Every day it sinks just a tiny bit more. If I don't find out what the problem is, my island will sink completely'.

Jack looked shocked.

"I'll help you find out what the problem is".

'You will?', but, before she could say any more, lightening came from the sky.

'Quick', said Laura, 'let's shelter in my cave'.

Jack shivered as they came across a big cave.

'It's quite dark!' said Laura, 'I'll put some lamps on'.

Jack wondered about his mum and Dad.

"Laura, my Mum and Dad will be worried. I ought to…."

She cut him off.

'Go, go back home, but please come back tomorrow'.
"I will. I'll be back soon after breakfast".
Jack set off, back to his boat and then home.

# Chapter 3
# The Close Escape

The next day Jack was up early. His mum had prepared him his usual breakfast of marmalade toast and milk. He ate quickly.

"I'm just going outside to play, I'm going to the beach" Jack said to his mum.

'OK, don't be late, and be careful playing by the sea, the tide can be very strong'.

"I will" shouted Jack, who was already half way to the barn at the bottom of the garden.

He pulled out the boat, sliding it across the soft sand, up to the waters edge. Jack set sail once again, happy and excited.

Soon, he shouted "I can see the island, LAURA, LAURA!" he cried at the top of his voice.

He reached the island but couldn't see Laura anywhere. He walked up the beach and stood under a palm tree.

"LAURA, LAURA" he called again.

Suddenly, a coconut fell on his head! Jack looked up to see a giggling monkey.

'Sorry' she said, still laughing. 'I dropped my coconut!'

Laura climbed down the tree and picked up the broken pieces of the coconut.

'I was just going to get some milk' she said, with a big cheeky smile.

"IT DID HURT!!" said Jack, trying not to sound too cross. (He didn't want to upset his new friend).

'Sorry', said Laura.

"Don't worry", said Jack.

He turned and started walking back down the beach.

"Right!" he said, "let's find out why this island is sinking!"

'Oh thank you Jack', shouted Laura as she jumped up and down clapping her hands, 'Thank you, thank you, thank you....'

Jack smiled.

They set of towards the other end of the island.

"We need to look under water to see why your island is sinking. This end of the island has deeper water and we should see more"

'Oh no!' said Laura, 'I don't swim very well!'

"I do!" claimed Jack, "I'm a good swimmer. I won first place in the school swimming gala".

Laura's face lit up.

"I'll go under now" he said, and jumped in without hesitation.

Laura looked worried.

'I didn't tell you about the sharks!!'

He didn't hear her.

Jack went deep under water. He swam down and down, looking into the deep dark water below. He could see a shadow in front of him. As he swam closer he realized it was a SHARK!!

Jack cried out, but instead of Laura hearing him, something else had heard his cry. Jack swam as fast as he could to get to the shore and away from the shark. It didn't work. The more he splashed, it attracted the shark and now he was being chased!

Help was on its way.

Jack was scared. The shark was hungry. It could swim faster than Jack and it was getting closer and closer.

Suddenly, something jumped out of the water. It was a Dolphin!

'Hurray' shouted Laura, as she watched from the beach.

The Dolphin bumped the shark with its nose, over and over until the shark gave up the chase and swam away.

The dolphin swam over to Jack.

"Thank you" said Jack, "you saved my life"

The dolphin squeaked and nodded her head. She took him back to the beach where Laura was waiting.

'Jack' said Laura, 'you're safe'.

"The dolphin saved me. That shark wasn't very friendly!"

'I was going to tell you that but you jumped in before I had the chance' smiled Laura with relief.

# Chapter 4
# The Submarine

Jack and Laura both agreed that it was too dangerous to swim with the sharks, which lived in the water around the island.

"We need a submarine" Jack said, looking around for anything that he could use. Laura agreed and they set to work building a submarine that would protect them from the sharks.

At the end of each day, Jack would sail home and return the next day with more wood and more nails from his dad's shed.

Jack and Laura worked hard on their submarine, and on the fourth day, it was finally finished.

'There', said Laura, 'good as new!'

They both stood back and admired their work. It looked fantastic. Just like the submarines Jack had seen in the books that his dad kept.

"Oh, yesssss….." said a voice from behind them. They turned, quickly and surprised to see a snake, slithering out from the trees that lined the beach.

'Where did you come from? How did you get on my island?" exclaimed Laura.

"You mean my island!" said the snake!

'YOUR ISLAND' shouted Jack, 'This is Laura's island, and I'm her friend'

"Oh no" hissed the snake, "I think you'll find it'ssssss mine"

'Prove it?' demanded Laura. "Were there coconut trees here when you came, cos I planted them so this was my island then and it still is!'

"You've proved your point" said the snake, "but I'm poisonous" he hissed, "I will squeeze you and bite you, you cannot beat me!"

The snake was very long, and much stronger than Jack and Laura. He slithered passed them towards the submarine they had just finished. He began to wind his body round and round and round the wooden submarine. He started to squeeze. Tighter and tighter his grip became. The wood started to crack and splinter and then…. With one big squeeze, the submarine broke into pieces. He turned to Jack and Laura, hissed, and then slid into the sea.

'That was a sea snake' said Laura, 'He is friends with the sharks'

"Look at our submarine" said Jack, "What are we going to do now?"

Laura and Jack were very upset. So upset that they didn't talk any more about the submarine.

"I'm sorry" said Jack.

'It's not your fault' replied Laura.

"I've got to go home now. I'll see you tomorrow"

'Maybe you could ask your parents if you could stay at a friend's tomorrow night…. and then come here.'

"I'll ask" and with that Jack set off back towards the boat, and home.

Back home, Jack went and sat with his mum in the lounge.

"Mum, is it ok if I stay out tomorrow night? My friend's are camping on the beach.

'Alright Jack, as long as the weather is fine, and you wrap up warm'

"In the morning you can play outside too, if you like" said dad.

The next morning, Jack packed his bags and said goodbye to his parents. "See you tomorrow, don't worry about me, I'll be fine"

He ran to his boat and set sail for the island. A short time passed and he got to the island, where Laura was waiting. "Its fine, I can stay tonight. I'll sleep in the cave".

'Great, so will I' said Laura.

They set up camp. Night came and they set down to sleep.

Laura was the first to wake.

'Wake up, wake up!' she shouted.

"aaahh" said Jack.

'Jack, Jack, you're having a bad dream, wake up!'

"hhhmm" moaned Jack, as he sat up.

'Don't worry Jack, what ever you dreamt wasn't real' said Laura, putting her arm round his shoulder.

"I dreamt that the island sank. It was horrible. Some dreams do come true, don't they? Laura?"

'Only good ones, not bad ones' She smiled then looked away.

They both sat up. A sudden squeaking noise came from the sea. "It's the dolphin, who saved me" shouted Jack. They walked out from the cave to see the cheerful dolphin smiling back at them. "Hello" cried Jack.

'Hi dolphin' shouted Laura.

The dolphin squeaked.

# Chapter 5
# A Problem!

The dolphin seemed to be trying to tell them something.

'Your dolphin is very nice' said Laura.

"Yes" said Jack, "but now let's find out why your island is sinking"

As they turned, they heard the dolphin again, squeaking and crying. She was tangled in fishing nets.

"Dolphin" cried Jack.

'Oh no' shouted Laura, 'this is a real problem, we've got to get her out or she will die'.

Laura and Jack started to think.

'How will we get her out?' worried Laura.

"I don't know" said Jack.

They looked around for things that they used to help.

'What about these broken pieces of coconut shell?' said Laura, as she bent down and picked up two big segments that were sticking out of the sand.

"How will that help?" asked Jack looking puzzled.

'Well, if we row out to the net in your boat, we should be able to cut through enough of the netting with the sharp edges of the coconut shell to free dolphin. It has to be worth trying!"

"What a great idea" shouted Jack, and he ran back to his boat.

"Grab all the coconut shells you can find" he called as he ran up the beach, "I'll get the boat."

A few minutes later, Jack arrived in the boat. Laura jumped in with at least five pieces of sharp coconut shell. They each took one oar and rowed out to meet dolphin in the net.

Both Jack and Laura reached over the side of the small boat and grabbed a handful of fishing net. They cut furiously at the net with the coconut shell until a hole started to appear.

"Keep going" shouted Jack, "its working!!"

Before long they had managed to cut a large enough hole for dolphin to escape. They dropped the net back into the water.

Dolphin squeaked and wriggled and wriggled towards the hole.

She was free!! She jumped out of the water, and then again, and again, squeaking with delight.

"We saved dolphin" cheered Jack, "dolphin is saved!"

Jack and Laura sat down in the boat.

"Now that dolphin is safe, we really need to find out about the island" said Jack.

'Yes' replied Laura, 'otherwise it may sink!'

# Chapter 6
# The Stranger!

That afternoon, Laura was picking coconuts while Jack was sitting under a tree, thinking about a way to solve this problem.

"I can't think of anything" he cried.

'Can't think of anything??' called a voice from behind.

Jack and Laura jumped up and looked round. They were surprised to see a wise looking grey rabbit sitting against a palm tree, looking very relaxed and sipping juice from a pineapple with a bamboo straw.

"Where did you come from?" asked Laura, raising her voice with surprise.

'I've been here since you arrived, monkey. I've lived here a long, long time' he told her.

"What's your name?" asked Jack.

'My name is Worry' replied the rabbit.

"I'm Laura, and this is my best friend, Jack. How did you get here Worry?"

'I'll tell you my story' said Worry, 'come and sit down'.

'When I was a baby rabbit, my owner took me sailing on their yacht. There was a bad storm one night and my owner was washed overboard. I was left on my own. The storm cleared and the boat floated to this island. I managed to get off before the tide took the boat back out to sea. I have lived here ever since.'

"WOW" shouted Laura, "that's fantastic!"

'It sounds amazing' claimed Jack.

"Fantastic, amazing and very lucky" said Worry, "but I am sad to have lost my owner. His name was Alan, and he took me to many wondrous places"

Jack, Laura and Worry talked and talked for at least an hour.

"I shall show you where I live" Worry shouted as he jumped up, "this way!"

They followed him through the trees, running quickly so they didn't lose him.

"Here we are" he shouted. It was a hole in the sand.

'So this is where you live?' said Jack, looking around him.

"Yes" said Worry.

# Chapter 7
# Solving the Problem!

Worry dived into the hole. A few seconds later he popped back up.

"So what were you talking about earlier?" he asked. "Something about a problem you wanted to solve?"

'We were talking about how we can solve the problem that Laura's island is sinking!'

"We have to go under the water to see what the problem is" said Laura.

"Jack almost got eaten by a shark when he went under before"

'Eaten by what?' inquired Worry.

"A Shark!"

'I was terrified' added Jack.

They talked late into the evening. It would soon be time for bed.

"What ever will I do without my island?" said Laura sadly, as she settled down to sleep.

'Well' said Worry, 'If Jack had a pole, he could use it to scare away the sharks, then he could see what was causing the island to sink. Sharks do not like a poke on the nose from a pointy pole."

'Sounds like a brilliant idea' said Laura, 'let's talk in the morning'.

They all set down for the night, cuddled together under the light of the silver moon, warmed by the gentle tropical breeze.

The next morning they all woke with the sun. They all hoped that this would be the day that they would find out why the island was sinking.

"I might be a bit scared!" said Jack, "but for Laura's island, I will do it".

'Can I go down with him?' Laura asked.

"We will all go down" said Worry as he handed out three bamboo poles.

All three friends jumped into the warm, clear water together.

It got darker the deeper they swam but they were comforted by the colourful reefs that surrounded them.

Suddenly…..

"SHARK!" cried Laura, "HELP!" she screamed.

Jack was close and pushed out his pole, poking the shark on the nose to scare it away.

"Thanks Jack" nodded Laura.

'This way to the bottom of the island' waved Worry.

Soon the colours of the reef began to disappear and it started to get darker. They were reaching the bottom of the island.

WOOOOOOO WOOOOOOOO

They all froze. A sound that they had never heard before was coming from below them. A sound like sad singing or crying was echoing through the water.

'Ssshh' said Jack.

Jack, Laura and Worry kept very, very still.

# Chapter 8
# The Whales

Just as Jack was about to speak, four huge whales swam out from under the island towards them.

"Wow" shouted Laura, "how fantastic."

As they wondered at the sight of such magnificent animals, Jack saw dolphin swimming with the whales.

'Dolphin' he called. The dolphin swam quickly towards them, happy to see his rescuers again.

'I'll see if dolphin can ask the whales what they're doing here' said Jack.

Dolphin swam to the whales. She squeaked and clicked. The whales squeaked and clicked back. They were deep in conversation.

"What are they saying?" said Laura.

'I don't know' said Jack, 'but they sound friendly!'

"Whales are always friendly" exclaimed Worry.

Dolphin swam over to Jack, Laura and Worry. The whales looked over and smiled. Dolphin swam up to Jack.

'The whales live under the island' she said.

"That must be why it is sinking" shouted Laura.

'They must be bumping against the bottom of the island and wearing it slowly away' claimed Jack. 'They do not realize that they are causing your island to sink'.

"We will have to find them another home" said Worry, "then Laura's island will be safe".

'How will we get them to go somewhere else?' said Laura, 'This is their home'.

"I know!" shouted Jack. "Dolphin, can you........?" Dolphin knew exactly what to do, squeaked, and dived into the open sea.

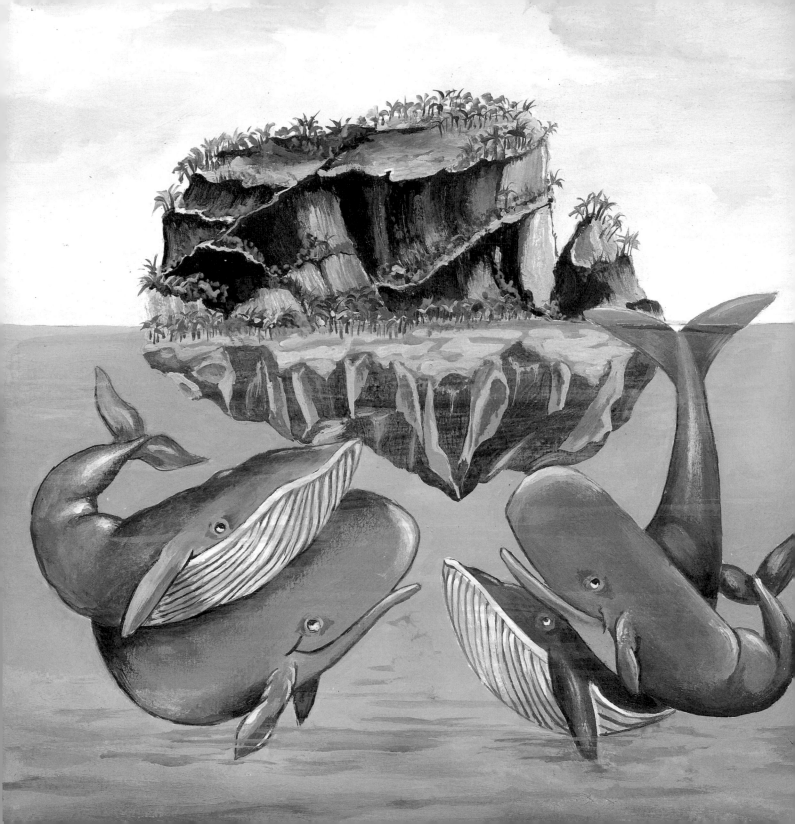

# Chapter 9
# The Plan

Dolphin swam to the whales and began squeaking and clicking in a language that only they understood. The whale family was clearly happy with their present home and did not wish to move.

Jack, Laura and Worry watched as the magnificent whales talked with the dolphin. Jack gazed at them. They were so big.

Suddenly the biggest whale turned and swam towards Jack, Laura and Worry.

"Oh no" cried Laura, as he bumped hard into the island, causing it to shake.

He couldn't speak like Laura, but she realized he was trying to say sorry for bumping the island and making it sink.

Laura looked at him kindly, "don't worry" she said, nodding her head. The whale smiled. "We will ask dolphin to find you another home. Then we can all be happy"

Dolphin swam off, into the deep dark water.

# Chapter 10
# A Happy Home

"If you hadn't come to my island, I would not have been able to save it" said Laura, excitedly. "If we can find a good home for the whales, the island will be safe and they will have a new home."

'This has been a great adventure!' replied Jack. 'I hope dolphin can find the whales a new home'.

A few minutes later, dolphin appeared at great speed and looking very excited.

'Squeak, squeak, click click squeak. CLICK CLICK, SQUEAK, SQUEAK!' she called to the whales, as she raced towards them. She jumped straight out of the water and did a double somersault before diving back in, just in front of the family of whales.

All the whales looked at each other with delight. They all began to roll over and over together and thrashed their tales up and down with glee.

"STOP, STOP!" cried Jack, "You're starting to rock Laura's island!"

The whales calmed down and swam, with dolphin, up to Jack Laura and Worry. They smiled and nodded as they glided past.

Dolphin had found them a new island to live under. An island with no animals or people living on it. An island that the whales could bump and rub against all day long. An Island with a big cave! The whales were thrilled!!

Jack, Laura and Worry waved to the whales and thanked dolphin again for his help. They swam back to their island.

# Chapter 11
# Back on the Island

Jack looked at Laura and smiled.

"Now the whales are happy and you have your island back, safe and sound"

'You are a real hero!' Laura said as she gave Jack a big hug, 'without you, this island may have sunk'.

"Thank you very, very much" added Worry, "We may have drowned without your help"

Jack smiled and stood up to face his friends.

"You are the best friends a boy could have. This has been an amazing adventure and I have had the best time, ever! But, my home is with my mum and dad and I really must go home now"

His head bowed as he turned to walk away.

'Well' said Worry, 'you've certainly had a good time'

Jack spun round and gave Worry a big hug. Then he turned to Laura.

"I'll visit you as often as I can" he said, nodding his head and smiling from ear to ear. "Maybe I'll bring some friends from home next time."

'That would be lovely' smiled Laura, 'now go, before you get in trouble.'

Jack waved to his friends, got into his boat, and set sail for home.

"Now I know what's in the middle of nowhere!" he said to himself, with a big, big smile.

# The End

# About the Author

Morgan Georgia Blanks is an inspirational story writer of extraordinary talent. Still only 9 years of age, she has the maturity and ability to write wonderful passages of adventurous writing that absorbs even the most articulate writers of modern children's books.

Morgan spends most of her spare time reading and writing to a level that commendably exceeds her peers.

With a love of theatre, performing arts and film, her imagination has been allowed to create characters and worlds that enthral and enlighten all who read her work.

She has quickly developed the ability to convey her imagination to paper so that we all may share in the fascinating lives of her characters.

By chance, Morgan was put in touch with local respected artist Sussi Arctander who has been painting all of her life and worked with children's stories before. With combined ambition and imagination they have achieved a quite enchanting story.

# About the Illustrator
# Susanne Arctander

The Danish born illustrator of this delightful story, has also been a successful artist on both sides of the Atlantic for quite some time.

Her varied career in the arts spans over 40 years in freelance design, furniture painting, commissioned pieces in landscape and portraiture.

Presently, Susanne continues to use her imaginative and unique talent as an Art Teacher

while still undertaking her great love of illustrating childrens books.

As a grand mother she finds her new found relationship with this young author, Morgan both delightful and inspirational.

Lightning Source UK Ltd.
Milton Keynes UK
UKRC01n2052060916
282384UK00009B/58

9 781434 390066